DATE DUE

MR 29 '96			
MY 30 '96			
AP 19 01			
MY 6 01			

DEMCO 38-296

BLAZING BLADERS

BLAZING BLADERS

THE WILD AND EXCITING WORLD OF IN-LINE SKATING

BILL GUTMAN

A TOM DOHERTY ASSOCIATES BOOK

BLAZING BLADERS

Cover photograph © 1992 by Shawn Frederick
Principal photographs © 1992 Shawn Frederick
Interior photographs listed as ski training,
racing, and drafting © 1992 Canstar Sports USA
Interior illustrations © 1992 Ben Brown
Book design by Fritz Metsch

A TOR BOOK
Published by Tom Doherty Associates, Inc.
175 Fifth Avenue
New York, N.Y. 10010

Tor® is a registered trademark of Tom Doherty Associates, Inc.

ISBN: 0-812-51939-6

First edition: May 1992

Printed in the United States of America

0 9 8 7 6 5 4 3 2 1

ACKNOWLEDGMENTS

For their help and contributions to *Blazing Bladers*,
Tor Books gives special thanks to:

Rollerblade, Inc.
Lynn Alpeter—Canstar Sports/Bauer
Kris Bowers—Oakley Inc.
Rhonda—Rector Inc.
Tracy—CCM/Maska

CONTENTS

INTRODUCTION

The premise is a simple one. A single line of three, four or five wheels positioned in the center of a lightweight, but sturdy and supportive boot. Put a pair on and you have entered the world of in-line skating, one of the newest and most exciting sports to come along in years. It's a sport that is practical, versatile and exciting, all at the same time.

In-line skating didn't begin to catch on until the latter 1980's, but in the 90's it is expected to be one of the fastest growing physical activities and sports in the country. Perhaps the main reason for the sudden and rapid growth of in-line skating is that the sport can be so many different things for different people.

For starters, it's a practical sport because it provides a low-impact, aerobic workout. There is much less pounding on the body, especially the legs, than there is with jogging or even cycling. Risk of injury is relatively minor. Unlike ice skating, an obviously close relative, an in-line skating workout can be had almost anywhere and on a number of different surfaces. You don't need a pond and sub-freezing weather, or an indoor, ice-covered rink.

"People are looking for alternatives to running and cycling," said one major retailer of in-line skates. "In-line skating is a low-impact sport that doesn't aggravate injuries. More and more of my customers are runners who come in with lower back pain."

The sport is versatile because of the number of different activities that skaters can pursue. They can simply skate for pleasure or for fitness. If they choose, however, they can advance to doing stunts (jumping, ramps), participate in roller-hockey, simulate downhill, cross country or slalom skiing; windsail, become involved in artistic dancing or just plain let it hang out and race. There seems to be no end to the number of activities available once a pair of in-line skates are laced up and in place.

As for excitement, well, that speaks for itself. An in-line skater with the skills to race, do stunts, jump, take hills or play hockey is participating in a sport of speed and thrills. Many in-line skaters have "crossed over" from other sports. Bicycle racers, skateboarders, skiers and snowboarders all look for the same rush of excitement on their in-line skates as they did in the other sports.

That, too, is the beauty of in-line skating or blading, as some prefer to call it. Athletes and participants in many other sports can enter the world of the single-blade (the name for the single row of wheels) skate and quickly transfer previously honed skills. Before long they are tearing it up as a blader, doing both old and new things on their skates.

In-line skating is a sport that is open to everyone. Youngsters from the age of four on up have learned how to use the skates. Conversely, senior citizens at 65 or 70 have found they are not yet too old to learn the basics of in-line skating. In fact, upwards of three million people have discovered they don't need two sets of wheels on a skate to enjoy themselves. Many have found that it is easier to adapt to the single blade than the conventional double-wheeled roller skate.

Newcomers to in-line skating can learn the basic skills quickly. However, they must first be educated about the sport, especially the safety aspect. Beginners must also be well aware of the protective equipment and gear they should be wearing whenever they don their skates. After that, all it takes is a couple of sessions with a qualified instructor or skilled blader and even beginners will be ready to go, ready to enjoy a whole new world of excitement that is in-line skating.

PART ONE

A BRIEF HISTORY OF IN-LINE SKATING

In-line skating is such a simple concept it's a wonder it didn't become popular long ago. There is evidence of some form of ice skating dating back several thousand years. The first ice skates were made of pieces of animal bone attached to the bottoms of boots. It made travel over the ice much easier than walking.

Ice skating as a sport began on the lakes of Scotland and within the canals of the Netherlands. By the 13th and 14th centuries, wood had replaced bone as the skate blade, with the first iron bladed skates manufactured in 1572. Yet while ice skating continued to modernize and grow, there were very few attempts to transfer the principle to a wheeled skate.

One recorded attempt was made in the early 1700's by a Dutchman, a man who loved ice skating and was looking for a way to find a similar activity for the summer months. Using materials he had on hand, he tried nailing wooden spools to strips of wood and then attached them to the bottoms of his shoes. Needless to say, he didn't go out to do half-pipes or take jumps. The idea did not catch on.

A number of years later, in 1760, an Englishman named Joseph Merlin also tried putting a line of wheels onto a pair of shoes. Merlin's skates could only go straight ahead. He quickly learned how important turning ability was when he skated straight into a huge mirror at the end of a ballroom as he was giving a demonstration.

There may have been some other rudimentary attempts at an in-line skate, but none really took hold. In 1819, a Frenchman named Petitbled invented a skate that had two, three or four wheels in a straight line. But once again the rigid construction of the skate made it impractical. A skater had all kinds of trouble maneuvering.

During this time, ice skating was flourishing the world over. Because so many people enjoyed skating on ice, there were still attempts to find a way to skate on flat land. That meant wheels or rollers of some kind. Finally, in 1863, an American named James Plimpton found a way to make a workable skate. He crafted a four-wheel skate with two pairs of wheels side by side. One pair was under the ball of the foot, the other pair under the heel. Thus the modern four-wheel roller skate was born.

Plimpton's skates made it possible to turn, as well as skate both forward and backwards. Pretty soon, the better skaters could copy all the movements of ice skaters. The invention of ball bearing wheels in 1884 helped the sport to grow even more.

With double-wheeled roller skating becoming more popular with the passage of time, the thought of a single row of wheels on a skate was largely forgotten. Suddenly, there didn't seem to be a need for in-line skates.

All that changed in 1980 when two brothers from Minnesota found themselves rummaging through a pile of equipment at a sporting goods store. Scott and Brennan Olson were ice hockey players and that's probably the reason they were interested when they stumbled on an old in-line skate. They suddenly had an old idea but in a new form. What if they could perfect a skate like this with just one row of wheels, a single "blade?" It would enable them to practice hockey during the summer months when there was no ice available.

Pumped up with excitement, they took the skate home and began working on the new design in their basement. Among other things, they used polyurethane wheels and added a rubber heel brake. Sure enough, the Olsons found they could maneuver on the new, in-line skates in much the same way they could maneuver on the ice. They had created a perfect tool for cross-training, making it possible to improve their hockey skills during the off-season and without ice.

It wasn't long before the brothers realized that the new skates were more than just a way to practice hockey. They were simply fun to use and gave them a great, low-impact workout. Why not, then, go into business? So they began making and selling the skates right out of their own home, first mainly to hockey players and skiers, then to others. They called their skates Rollerblades® and before long, Rollerblade, Inc., was born. It was the first company in the world to manufacture in-line skates and is still the leader in a growing field today.

THE LURE OF IN-LINE SKATING

SkateSmart is a new campaign that was started by five in-line skate manufacturers in mid-1991. It reflects the amazingly rapid growth of the sport. Whenever a sport grows as quickly as in-line skating there are always safety concerns, especially when the growth is so dynamic that there might not be enough qualified instructors around. The National Sporting Goods Association estimated that there were more than three million in-line skaters on the roads, hills, streets and playgrounds of the country in 1991. With the lure of this exciting sport increasing rapidly, those involved felt they had to organize.

The result was the formation of the International In-Line Skate Association (IISA).

"Because of this rapid growth, there is an abundance of

newcomers to the sport who are hungry for information on how to get started and what to do with their new skates," said Joe Janasz, national director of IISA. "Although in-line skating is easy and exciting to learn, the manufacturers want skaters to take the time to learn how to use the skates properly."

Janasz goes on to say that people should "follow a few simple rules, respect the rights of other outdoor enthusiasts and use a little common sense."

As part of their campaign to educate and monitor newcomers to the sport, SkateSmart has developed 10 Rules of the Road for all in-line skaters. Before discussing the sport further, here are the IISA rules for bladers as they were originally written.

1. Wear protective gear including a helmet, knee and elbow pads, and wrist guards.
2. Achieve a basic skating level before taking to the road.
3. Stay alert and be courteous at all times.
4. Always skate under control.
5. Skate on the right side of paths, trails and sidewalks.
6. Overtake pedestrians, cyclists and other skaters on the left.
7. Stay away from water, oil or debris on the trail, and uneven or broken pavement.
8. Observe all traffic regulations.
9. Avoid areas with heavy automotive traffic.
10. Always yield to pedestrians.

While each of these rules will be discussed more fully throughout the balance of the text, it's important that any in-line skater be aware of them and familiarize himself or herself with each one before putting on the skates for the first time. The rules of the road represent step one to enjoying life as a skater.

But the lure of the sport goes way beyond a set of rules. It goes back to what was touched on earlier, the maneuverability, practicality and versatility of the sport. Take the case of Bruce Jackson, for example. Today, the California-based 28-year-old is a professional in-line skater. He is one of the senior members of Team Rollerblade®, a group of in-line skaters who represent both their company and the sport, serving as roving ambassadors to demonstrate the fun and excitement of in-line skating. Yet he began to skate simply to try to improve his hockey skills.

"I grew up in the Los Angeles area playing basketball and participating in gymnastics," Jackson said. "As I got older, I began playing ice hockey. When I bought my first pair of in-line skates in 1987 my idea was simply to train with them as a hockey player.

"But soon I began doing other things on the skates. I applied gymnastics and dance skills to my skating and began to develop a lot of moves on my own. When I took my skates to the beach they were always a conversation piece. People would tell me I was a cool dude on the skates and everyone seemed interested in them. Then I met a man named Chris Morris who worked for Rollerblade and suggested that I begin teaching for them. I finally agreed."

Jill Schultz, another senior member of Team Rollerblade, was a professional figure skater and dancer. Like Bruce Jackson, she is California-based and began in-line skating at the beach. Within two years, her reputation as an in-line skater was so widespread that she was asked by Rollerblade to begin giving demonstrations and to help newcomers learn how to skate. It wasn't long before Jill also began to notice the lure in-line skating had for many different people.

"I was a figure skater and the technical training I had allowed me to do many of the same things very quickly on in-line skates. The same would apply to people from many other sports. Downhill skiers, for instance, will usually began taking hills shortly after starting to skate. Someone who is used to performing on ramps with a skateboard or BMX bike will get on a pair of in-line skates and quickly excel on ramps.

"People coming over from running or aerobics will use the skates for the same kind of workouts. Figure skaters always ask me what kinds of jumps they can do with in-line. That's what is so great about in-line skating. People come over from another sport and begin doing the same type of thing right away.

But before long they find out they can do everything else on the skates, as well.

"I can keep practicing my figure skating, for example. But I can also go downhill, skate ramps, do ski gates like a slalom skier or simply compete in races. So in-line skating offers something for everyone and a lot of different things for many of those people as well."

As the sport continues to grow, it is becoming increasingly organized. There are more races being held in more cities, the skaters competing in 5-kilometer, 10K and even 30K distances. Stunt competitions and organized rollerhockey leagues are springing up all over, while the recreational use of in-line skates also grows.

"I knew in-line skating was here to stay when I saw a guy with a suit and tie, carrying a briefcase, rolling down Fifth Avenue in New York City," said Jeff Kabat, who sells the skates in the Big Apple.

Commuting to work may not be the most common use of in-line skates, but it is just part of the boom that has definitely arrived during the past several years. For those who like to drop names, add singer-dancer Janet Jackson and motion picture superstar Arnold Schwarzenegger to the list of people who enjoy the blazing blades in their spare time.

In-line skates have also been endorsed by the Boston Bruins, a professional ice hockey team; and by the United States Ski Team. Both groups obviously have found blading to be an ideal cross-training tool. So the lure of the sport is everywhere.

Recreational skaters have a whole variety of reasons for taking up blading. A 28-year-old female textile consultant in St. Louis loves the results she sees after a series of skating workouts.

"I love it because it tones my lower body," she said, "and that's just where I need it."

A Marietta, Ohio, warehouse supervisor found in-line skating an aerobic exercise that didn't put excessive wear on his body.

"It's a graceful, flowing activity," was the way he put it. "I have bad knees and can't jog. Plus it beats stair climbing as well as jogging because you can go farther faster, and with less pounding."

A female law student at the University of Chicago views in-line skating as just plain fun.

"The whole lakefront in Chicago is covered with bladers," she said. "Every weekend it's a battle between the cyclists and the bladers."

Yet the appeal of in-line skating may eventually be most attractive to another whole generation of skaters, the young city kids who are finding out the many things they can doing when they hit the pavement with their blades. As Bruce Jackson put it:

"Kids are really taking to it. They know they're developing a new sport and they consider it their sport. They think they own it."

PART TWO

GETTING READY TO SKATE

People who have already participated in sports such as ice skating, roller skating, skateboarding and skiing can usually make an easy transition to in-line skating. Because it's not difficult to learn to use a pair of in-line skates, those with a sports background can sometimes just put the skates on, receive some basic instruction, and Go! But real beginners, whether six or 60, should have some knowledge of the sport ahead of time.

In fact, even experienced athletes ready to tackle blading should be completely familiar with the equipment, with the rules of safety, possible pitfalls and common injuries, and the need for general physical fitness before taking off.

THE SKATE

Since you can't hit the pavement without a pair of skates, that has to be the first item a new skater must purchase. Good in-line skates are not cheap. Prices for quality equipment can range from $80 to $400, depending on the size and model. As with some other sports, the first rule of thumb is to buy the best possible skates you can afford.

The in-line skate is a rather unique piece of equipment. Unlike many ice skates and roller skates, which are mounted under a rather flimsy leather boot, the in-line boot is much lighter and sturdier, similar to a ski boot. The leather boot gives little ankle support. That's why so many first-time ice skaters find their ankles turning as soon as they hit the ice.

A good in-line boot is made from molded polyurethane or a co-polymer plastic. Both materials are lightweight, but extremely sturdy. The lateral support on a top-quality in-line skate is nothing short of amazing. While a new skater might find his knees wobbling a bit when he first stands on the skates, his ankles will feel steady as a rock.

One word of caution. Some boots are made out of a material called polyethylene, which people can easily confuse with polyurethane. A simple test is to squeeze the boot hard. If it feels soft or pliable, then it is not made from top-notch material and won't give you the steady-as-a-rock ankle support just mentioned.

Getting the proper fit with a boot is also very important. Both too tight and too loose can cause problems. The ideal fit is a snug one with the laces also snugged up. When you stand up on the skates your toes should not jam into the front of the boot. They can touch very slightly, giving you a little needed extra room. When you bend your knees and your toes drop back slightly, they should not feel cramped by the sides of the boot.

Another innovation new skaters can look for is the "hinged cuff." The cuff is the top part of the skate and the hinged version allows a full range of motion when you skate. It also makes it much easier for the skater to keep his weight forward.

Skates should be tried on with the same kind of socks you plan to wear when actually skating. Don't go in with a pair of dress socks under your shoes and try on a pair of in-line skates. Another word of caution. A regular thick cotton sock will not keep the feet dry. Perspiration buildup can promote blisters and general foot discomfort. Bladers should consider wearing either a thin undersock make of silk or polypropylene, or a specially padded athletic sock.

The first type can be worn under a medium-weight athletic sock and will aid in absorbing perspiration. The padded sock helps prevent blisters and also helps keep the foot dry, even during a vigorous workout on a hot day.

A good pair of in-line skates will also help prevent the buildup of excess moisture. The older model skates were basically one solid piece of material. Some of today's boots are made with vents to allow liberal air circulation. These "breathable" skates will also feel more comfortable, especially during that hot weather workout just mentioned.

Other advantages of a high-quality skate include its lighter weight and a foam liner to cushion the foot. A lighter-weight skate will give the skater a bit more ease of performance, while the foam cushion conforms to the foot and further reduces the impact from the skating surface. The foam cushion is also available as an insert and can be put into a less expensive skate. If you can't afford a high-quality skate as a beginner the cushion insert would be a worthwhile investment.

There are many different in-line skate models available. Some of the smaller skates for youngsters have just three wheels. The majority of bladers, however, use a four-wheel model. This can be considered the standard skate on which almost all in-line skating activities can be achieved. There is also a five-wheel model, but that is more of a specialized skate, extremely fast, and used mainly for racing. Five-wheel skates should be used only by experienced skaters with advanced technique. More on them later.

CARE AND MAINTENANCE OF YOUR SKATES

The frame on which the wheels sit should not twist or turn to any great degree. A slight torque is all right, but if it twists too much the skate will be unstable. The best frames are made out of nylon, reinforced with fiberglass. Check the frame from time to time to make sure it isn't getting loose. The good ones shouldn't.

Wheels are made of polyurethane, and along with the brake, need periodic inspection and maintenance. The boot and frame simply have to be kept clean and that can be done by wiping them with a soft damp cloth after use. But the wheels are a different story.

Though polyurethane is a tough material, skating on cement, gravel or another rough surface is going to cause the wheels to wear. Wheel life can be extended by turning and rotating them, much the same way you would rotate the tires on a car.

There is no set formula for when to rotate the wheels. Much depends on the kind of usage you give your skates and also the types of surfaces upon which you do most of your skating. At one time it was suggested to rotate the wheels after a certain amount of miles. But now the general formula is to rotate them as soon as they begin wearing unevenly. If the wheels begin to look lopsided to your eye, get out the wrenches and go to work.

A blader doesn't have to be a mechanic to rotate his wheels. He will need two basic tools—an Allen wrench and a socket wrench. Most of the better skates require a 5/32 Allen wrench and a 7/16 socket. Beginner's skates take two 1/2 inch wrenches. The rule of thumb on the four-wheel skate is to change the wheel nearest the toe with the third wheel back, and rotate the second wheel from the front with the rear wheel. Also, when rotating, always turn the wheels so the side with the most wear is facing out. More wear occurs on the inside of the wheels from pushing off, striding and turning.

With the three-wheel skate, the front wheel should be moved to the rear, with the other two wheels moved up one notch toward the front. With the five-wheel racing skate, the front wheel is normally left in place, though it can be turned to keep the wear evenly. The next four wheels can be rotated using the same formula suggested for the four-wheel models. When putting the wheels in their new positions, tighten them until there is some resistance when they spin. Then loosen them bit by bit until they spin freely with no resistance.

How long wheels will last depends, of course, on the frequency of usage as well as the type of surface. Some bladers find they need a new set of wheels every month or two. Others can go a year or more before the wheels have to be replaced. A skater will know when he needs new wheels. He will find his skates slowing down and not responding as quickly when he goes to make his moves. It will feel as if the skates are fighting him. That's when it's time for a new set of wheels.

The bearings upon which the wheels spin rarely need maintenance. They should be wiped off if they get foreign substances such as oil, sand or even water on them. The better skates have bearings that are sealed and will not need lubrication. But it is still a good idea to wipe them down if they get soiled. Good bearings will last through several sets of wheels.

There is one other type of adjustment possible on some skate models. It's called "rockering" the wheels. A skate with rockered wheels simply means that the middle two wheels of a four-wheel skate or the middle wheel of a three-wheel skate are lowered slightly. Rockered wheels give an experienced skater added maneuverability for turning and pivoting. Rollerhockey players who have to move quickly in every direction will often rocker their wheels.

Since all skates come with their wheels flat, the skater must make the rockering adjustment. This can be done by removing the wheels to be rockered (the middle two or middle one). Then simply turn over the frame spacers in the holes of the wheel cavity of the frame. By turning the spacers, they will sit higher, though the opening is set so the axle will still fit through. The wrenches with which to make this adjustment always come with skates that can be rockered.

The brake is the other part of the skate that has to be watched. Bruce Jackson, for one, feels that stopping is the most difficult thing to learn on in-line skates and he describes the brake as "pure gold. The brake on the skates is fantastic, the most unbelievable tool on the skate."

If a top skater feels that way about the brake, it is obviously something every skater must watch. The brake is generally behind the wheel of the right skate, though some models do have a brake on both skates. For years, brakes were made of rubber. However, there is a new polyurethane brake that was available on some models in the fall of 1991. A skater must simply watch how quickly the brake wears, no matter from which material it is made. Once he finds himself having to make a 45-degree angle with his skate to get good brake contact, it is time to put on a replacement. As with a car, don't let the brake become too worn.

It's a good idea to get into the habit of checking your skates each time you use them. Make sure the frame is tight and that none of the wheels have loosened up. Also check the wear on your wheels. If you feel they need rotating, do it. And check the wear on the brake. When you have to stop, you want to be sure that brake is there.

CLOTHING AND PROTECTIVE EQUIPMENT

It cannot be emphasized enough that everyone from beginners to experts should skate smart. That doesn't mean throwing on a pair of shorts, a tee shirt and your skates, and just taking off. In-line skaters can achieve speeds upwards of 30 miles per hour and also do a variety of tricks and stunts. Even beginners can sometimes find themselves caught on a downward grade or hill, going even faster, and unsure how to stop. The possibility of a fall or wipeout always exists. So it pays to be protected.

As in many other sports, protection begins with a helmet. This is an absolute must for youngsters and beginners, and should also be worn by older, experienced skaters, especially if they are into tricks or hot-dogging. Hockey players, of course, must also wear helmets.

A good helmet will be comfortable, lightweight and tough. Many are made out of fiberglass and are lined with foam padding. Helmets are also vented to allow skaters to keep cool on a hot day. In addition, there is also a junior helmet made of a vented polystyrene soft shell and with a nylon mesh cover. This is a one-size-fits-all model that kids can wear for both in-line skating and biking.

For the very young and for older skaters, a helmet is a must. For those in between, including advanced skaters, it is still a highly-recommended piece of equipment.

Other important pieces of protective clothing include wrist and hand guards, elbow and knee pads. Since no one is completely immune from falling, this extra gear can help stop and soften a multitude of bumps and bruises, and in some cases maybe even a broken bone.

The majority of in-line skating falls (especially with beginners) involve the skater pitching forward during an attempted or too sudden stop. The natural instinct is to break the fall with the hands. That's why hand and wrist injuries are among the most common for bladers.

A good wrist guard for an in-line skater is a lot more than simply wearing a sweat band around the wrist. The standard guard has plastic inserts on both sides of the guard to stabilize the wrist in a fall. They are snugged up with an adjustable velcro strap for a tight fit. There is also a professional quality wrist guard on the market for stunt skaters, made from an even stronger material. Both wrist guards also offer some protection to the palms of the hands.

For additional protection a blader can wear a wrist wrap skating glove that has a padded palm. A good glove is made of leather, is fingerless and also reinforces the lower part of the wrist. The standard glove is nearly the same without the wrist wrap. Either glove will give the palms of the hands added protection if they are used to break a fall.

Elbow and knee pads speak for themselves. They are flexible and sometimes even interchangeable. Some basic knee and elbow guards are padded with a material of dense foam, while others have a tough, nylon plastic cap for extra protection. The knees and elbows are often points of impact during a fall and a skater will be thankful on more than one occasion that he remembered to wear his protective gear.

Like the skates, all protective gear requires minimum maintenance. Just make sure the gear is kept clean and inspect it regularly for signs of tears, worn velcro straps or looseness of any kind. With care, it should last a long time.

In a recent newspaper article on in-line skating in New York City, it was reported that on one summer weekend Lenox Hill Hospital treated 17 skating-related injuries. Also, a hand injury specialist, Dr. Richard Eaton of St. Clare's/Roosevelt Hospital in New York City, reported that he had seen some badly shattered wrists that were the result of in-line skating falls.

This is not to say that blading is an extremely dangerous sport or that people should be discouraged from trying it. On the contrary, because it is a new sport, people often jump into it without paying attention to all the safety rules. They get on their skates and before they know it are moving extremely fast without the proper technique to stop and/or turn. Daredevil types will also sometimes rush into stunt skating—jumping boxes, skating ramps—before they are really ready.

There is certainly a risk involved in skating, just as there is a risk involved in playing football, biking, skateboarding, skiing or even playing soccer. Team or individual sport alike, there is always the risk of an injury. The trick is to minimize the chance of injury by adhering to all safety rules and also learning what to do in a crisis.

"Your average in-line skater really tends to want to push it," explains Bruce Jackson of Team Rollerblade. "That's one thing about an in-line skater. It's so much fun that you want to do more and more and more of it. I've seen that time and again just being around bladers and teaching so many people.

"Beginners must get comfortable on their skates first. Once they're comfortable, that's when they want to go. But that's also the point they should slow down and learn all the techniques properly, in other words, take it one step at a time."

Jackson also confirmed what the doctors had said, that the biggest injury risk is to the wrist because the natural reaction is to reach out with the hands to break a fall. Most elbow and knee injuries are the bruising type and occur when people are not wearing their pads. He said that there are very few broken legs, and a minimal amount of knee injuries involving cartilage and ligament damage. Jackson's advice to beginners is simple.

"If you feel you're going to fall, don't fight it. The more you fight it, the harder you're going to fall. Relax, go down to your knees, then roll or dive over. The best way is to try to roll over on your shoulder. Turn as you fall. Instead of falling straight forward, try to roll to the right or left. That way, you're not going straight down and breaking the fall with your hands, wrists and arms."

Now it's understandable why Jackson has said the brake on an in-line skate is the most important tool a blader has. There will be details on using the brake in a subsequent chapter. Suffice to say here, intelligent use of the brake will enable a skater to avoid many of the pitfalls awaiting him out there.

Another obvious pitfall is skating down hills. Beginners may not realize how fast they will pick up speed or how difficult it is to stop.

"Beginners must absolutely avoid hills until they really know how to stop well," says Jill Schultz of Team Rollerblade. "Just getting a quick lesson on the use of the heel brake is not enough. It takes practice for someone to really be able to use it well. Bladers should also know alternate techniques to stop and slow down when skating a hill."

Schultz also said that other pitfalls for skaters include slick surfaces, such as water, oil, sand, ice or snow, as well as cracks in the pavement or skating surfaces.

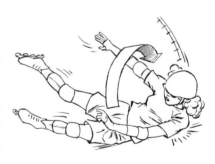

FALL

"If there is a lengthwise crack in the sidewalk or anything that runs parallel to your blade, you always want to cross it at an angle," she explained. "If the blade falls right in a crack you can easily be tripped up. In-line skates will surprise you by pretty much going over any rough surface or even over cracks and bumps. Just remember that the cracks can't be parallel to the blade."

Oil, water and sand are a different story. Any wet, slippery or sandy surface should be avoided whenever possible.

"A good analogy with oil, water, ice or snow is that they will cause you to slip on in-line skates much the same when they would if you were on a bicycle," said Jill Schultz. "If you can't avoid these surfaces just make sure you go through them slowly and on a straight line. It might even be a good idea to intentionally skate through a wet surface some time just to learn how much you can push. Just make sure you have your protective gear on.

"If you're prepared, a slippery surface probably won't trip you up. Problems arise when you're skating fast and come upon something unexpectedly. That's when you're likely to have an accident."

That's also the reason the SkateSmart campaign has created the Rules of the Road, outlined in the previous chapter. They basically urge all skaters to wear all their protective gear and to learn the techniques of skating before taking off on the open road.

There is also increasing concern that with the proliferation of in-line skaters in the big cities that there will be problems with automobiles as well as with pedestrians. The Rules of the Road implore bladers to observe all traffic regulations, to avoid areas with heavy automobile traffic and to always yield to pedestrians.

"Some towns and cities are already designating areas where bladers can and can't go," said Jill Schultz. "That's why we are putting so much emphasis on safety. We don't want to see the sport restricted.

"However, kids have to realize that if they want to skate everywhere they have to be courteous and must respect other people and their property. If a blader wants to do stunts, like skating stairs or walls, they have to realize they can't skate up storefront walls or jump off stairs on private property.

"Sometimes they get carried away and think they can go through the center of town and skate over everyone's personal property. That's where you run into situations where skating can be banned. Adults should explain things to the youngsters, tell them the reasons they can do everything. Kids can find empty parking lots or cul-de-sacs where there is little traffic and then can build their ramps or get cardboard boxes to jump."

So there is more to in-line skating than simply putting on your blades and skating off into the sunset. Serious injuries are not common, but they can happen. The best way to avoid them is to wear protective equipment at all times and to be aware of the pitfalls that are out there. Beginners should take pains to learn the techniques of the sport thoroughly before trying stunts or maneuvers that are geared for advanced skaters.

Maybe the best analogy is this. A little leaguer wouldn't want to face a Nolan Ryan fastball. A 12-year-old basketball player couldn't rebound with David Robinson or stop Michael Jordan from driving to the hoop. A Pop Warner football player wouldn't want to try to run through a National Football League defensive line. At the same time, a newcomer to in-line skating wouldn't want to put on his skates for the first time and suddenly find himself racing down a hill at 30 miles per hour or more.

Skate smart and skate safe. That's the best advance any blader can have.

FITNESS AND TRAINING

In-line skating, in itself, is great exercise and a great conditioner. As mentioned earlier, it is called a low-impact workout because there is virtually no pounding on the lower extremities—the hips legs, knees, ankles and feet. The various injuries that runners and joggers often have—knee pain, sore ankles, shin splints, blistered feet—virtually do not exist with in-line skating.

Dr. David Gilchrist, after studying the effects of in-line skating, noted in *The Physician and Sportsmedicine Journal* that "the skating motion used is like that in cross-country skiing, where you seldom encounter knee injuries or other lower-extremity injuries common to running."

His thesis was embellished a bit by Dr. James Garrick, an orthopedic surgeon at the Center for Sports Medicine at St. Francis Memorial Hospital in San Francisco.

"In-line skating," said Dr. Garrick, "seems to build quadriceps strength and endurance, and because of its low-impact is a good exercise for persons with knee problems."

Shape Magazine, a journal of mind and body fitness for

women, reached similar conclusions. It stated that in-line skating was an ideal cross-training tool for those who regularly engage in high-impact "pounding" sports such as running and jogging. The magazine also said that "in-line skating tones and firms leg and back muscles and is one of the few sports besides cross-country skiing that tones the inside of your quadriceps and gluteal muscles."

In addition, the magazine went on to say that the sport also had a way of reducing stress. Diana McNab, an advisory board member for *Shape,* put it this way.

"It (in-line skating) puts you in a flow state like nothing else, and the rhythm, tempo and timing is a real rejuvenator for a stressful day. You're outside, with the wind in your face, enjoying the cadence of running with none of the jarring or bouncing. You go into a sort of trance that creates a slow state rush."

Without getting too philosophical, blading is simply a great workout. Any injuries will occur either through a fall or perhaps by trying advanced stunts, which always have an element of risk. But the act of simply skating, no matter how fast or how far, will not normally result in injury because of the low-impact nature of the workout.

One of the other major benefits of in-line skating is what it does for the cardiovascular system. In other words, in-line skating is also a great aerobic activity that strengthens the heart and improves lung function. Skating also develops hip and thigh muscles that are not exercised to a great extent in running or cycling, and also works the hamstring muscles at the rear of the thigh that are not strengthened by cycling.

Of course, to achieve the cardiovascular benefits from in-line skating, you must follow a prescribed program of regular skating. This is the same as in running, cycling, swimming, cross country skiing or any other potential aerobic exercise.

For general fitness, it is advisable to skate a slow warm-up for five minutes, then skate at a steady but moderate pace for some 20 minutes, before skating a five-minute slow cool down. This should be done three or four times a week and is a basically minimum workout.

Intensity of the workouts can vary depending on the goal of the skater. For example, someone who is bent on losing weight and maybe controlling their level of stress should skate between four and six times a week for 45 to 60 minutes. The increased frequency and level of the workout will burn more calories and result in better weight control.

The smoothness of in-line skating can sometimes limit the intensity of workouts. So for those who might want to take their aerobic fitness even further, it is advising for them to skate up hill for a good part of their workout. However, skaters should only do this after becoming familiar with the techniques of hill climbing and also going downhill. For usually after a long climb up a hill, there is a return trip down.

In-line skating, in itself, can serve as a fine fitness tool. However, there is also a proper way to get ready to skate and ways to maintain general fitness for the entire body, not only the muscles toned and strengthened by skating. Let's start with the preparation for a blading workout.

In many other sports, the first order of business in warming up is to stretch, loosen the muscles that are going to be used for the workout. For in-line skating, a pre-workout stretch is not recommended.

"This is very important, especially for someone who isn't extremely active and who skates maybe once a week," explains Bruce Jackson. "That person should definitely not stretch his muscles as a first step. There are people who stretch first, think they are all warmed up, and then take off on their skates. This is wrong and can lead to injury.

"The reason is that with in-line skating, the body uses many muscles that simply cannot be stretched with conventional stretching exercises."

The recommended way to warm up is to put the skates on and then take a very slow, smooth warm-up skate of at least five minutes in duration. At the end of five minutes, it might even be a good idea to increase speed gradually before getting into any fast, explosive-type moves.

"By using the slow skate as a warm-up device, you are actually stretching and warming up those muscles that will be used specially for blading and for the fast, more explosive skating you are about to do," Jackson explained.

However, when the workout or skating session is over, things change. Now, it's time to stretch. As with other sports, the muscles are now fully warmed up and maybe even a bit fatigued. By stretching now, you can keep them loose and strengthen them at the same time. This does not necessarily mean the muscles you were told not to stretch beforehand, but rather a general stretching of all the major muscle groups.

The most important parts of the body to work on are the legs, lower back and the abdomen. The legs, of course, are instrumental to blading and cannot be ignored. The harder you work on your leg strength and flexibility, the more it will help your skating. In addition, because you are leaning forward while on your skates, there is also tension on the lower back muscles, as well as the muscles of the abdomen. In fact, lower back strength is often dependent on abdominal muscle strength, so any blader should spend the same amount of time stretching and strengthening both the lower back and the abdomen.

The following are a number of stretching exercises that will help keep this areas of the body supple and fit. They are by no means the only stretching exercises, just some basic ones to get you started.

Stretching exercises should always be done slowly, without any quick or herky-jerky motions. When any muscle is being stretched is should be held in the stretched position for a number of seconds rather than stretched and released quickly. Some suggest holding a stretch for as long as 60 seconds. It should be held at least 15 to 20 seconds, longer if it feels comfortable. Get into the maximum stretch position slowly, then back off at the first sign of pain. You should be able to feel the muscle stretching, but it shouldn't be painful. Once you get into a regular stretching program, you should be able to increase the maximum stretch position as the muscle becomes stronger and most elastic.

One other piece of advice. If you are involved in a regular stretching program and want to stretch when you have no plans

LEG STRETCH

to skate, it is still not a good idea to begin stretching cold muscles. If you can put your skates on and just take the slow, five-minute warm-up skate, do that. If not, you might want to warm up by jogging in place for a few minutes or doing an exercise such as jumping jacks. You might even jog slowly around the block or around the house a couple of times. This will serve as the same kind of warm-up as the five-minute skate and get the muscles ready for stretching.

HAM STRETCH

You can begin working your legs with a basic hamstring stretch. There are two ways to do this. One way is to stand before a bar or bench about waist high. Then place one leg on the support, keeping it straight. Bend the other leg at the knee just slightly. Then lean forward slowly, sliding your hands down the leg that is on the support. As the hands approach the foot, you will feel the hamstring muscle stretch. Hold the position for 20 seconds, then straighten up slowly. Switch legs and do it again. This stretch can be done five times with each leg.

A similar stretch can be done why lying on your back. Bend one leg until your foot is alongside the knee of your extended leg. Then raise the extended leg, keeping the feet relaxed. As the leg comes up, put your hands around your calf or as high as you can reach and help pull the leg toward you until you feel the hamstring stretch. Hold the position for 20 seconds or more, then slowly release it. Next bend that leg up until the foot is alongside the knee of your other leg. Then stretch that one.

STRETCH

Again alternate until you have stretched each leg five times.

An exercise that works both the hamstring and the lower back is commonly known as the hurdler's stretch. It is done by sitting on the floor with your legs spread wide apart in front of you. One leg is then folded back tucked tight to the buttocks. Next bend forward from the waist moving your hands towards the outstretched leg. Stretch as far as you can without feeling pain, then hold it for 20 seconds. Next reverse the position of your legs and repeat it on the other side.

Another good stretching exercise is called the lunge. This one stretches not only the hamstrings, but also the quadriceps in the front of the thigh and the gluteus muscles in the but-

LUNGES

CALF STRETCH

QUAD STRETCH

BACK STRETCH

tocks. It is done by placing one leg in front of you, the toe in front of the knee. Then slowly bring the other leg directly back, sinking into the lunge position until the calf and thigh of the front leg are at a 45-degree angle and the back leg is stretched back as far as it will go, maintaining balance on your toe. You will feel the stretching in the leg and buttocks as you hold the position. Then return to a standing position and reverse the leg action.

Calves can be stretched by standing about two feet from a wall. Then place your hands on the wall and move both feet back until they are in a position where you can still place your whole foot on the floor. The further away from the wall you move your feet, the more stretch you will feel in the calves. This can be done with one leg at a time, or with both at one time. Again, hold the maximum stretch for about 20 seconds.

A good quad stretch is simply done by holding a chair, rail or even the wall for balance, then raising one foot behind you and grabbing your shin with your hand. Now pull your foot back toward the buttocks until you feel the stretching in your quadriceps. Hold the position the usual amount of time, then repeat with the other leg. Again, stretch each leg about five times.

Another good way to stretch back muscles is to lie on a flat surface. Then raise one leg at the knee, put your hands around the calf just below the knee and pull the leg up as tight to your stomach as you can without pain. Hold the position the usual time, then repeat it with the other leg. This exercise will stretch and loosen all the back muscles.

Stomach muscles can be strengthened with conventional sit-ups. Just make sure you do them with knees bent. Never do a sit-up with your legs straight out in front of you. That puts too much strain on the lower back.

There are undoubtedly other stretching exercises that can be done, as well. Check with a coach or even another blader to see what his routine might be. Using the aforementioned exercises and others, you should be able to work up a valuable and necessary stretching routine.

It has already been established that in-line skating is an

outstanding aerobic exercise, as well as an exercise that strengthens and tones the legs. As part of a total fitness program, a blader should also take some time to exercise his upper body. There are a number of ways to do this, including a couple of tricks that can be done with the in-line skates.

To tone and strengthen the arms and shoulders, a skater can carry some light weights in his hands while he skates. There are weights called "heavy hands" that have been used by runners for years. They can easily be held while skating and should not affect a skater's balance or maneuverability. They may just make him tire a bit sooner.

Another method is to get a set of ski poles and emulate the motions of cross-country skiing while on your blades. Again you'll be swinging your arms and shoulders in a rhythmic pattern and adding a small weight (the poles) to the overall package.

1. SKATER WITH CROSS-COUNTRY POLES

Otherwise, it might be a good idea to add a few upper body toning and strength exercises to your stretching routine. The simplest standbys are push-ups and pull-ups, both of which can be done easily and even between stretching exercises. They will build up the arms and shoulders. Bladers can also get into a routine weight-lifting program, either with the newer machines on the market or with old-fashioned free weights.

As is the case with any kind of new form of exercise or sport, those beginning a weight program should get some solid advice from a knowledgeable person or coach. Tell them about your sport and what you want from the weight program. They should be able to suggest the right exercises and the frequency with which you should do them.

Good general fitness is something everyone should strive to achieve. But for someone who want to get heavily involved with in-line skating, it is a real necessity. Stretching and general fitness can only help you avoid injuries and become a better blader along the way.

PART THREE

THE BASICS OF IN-LINE SKATING

STARTING TO SKATE

Where do you start? Do you just go out and buy a pair of in-line skates, put them on and and hit the pavement? Perhaps someone crossing over from ice skating or roller skating, skateboarding or skiing can do it, but a beginner cannot. Even experienced athletes from other sports need some basic technique and definitely must know how to stop. But the beginner should take it step by step, and that is the purpose of this chapter.

You've already got your skates. They fit well. You're wearing the right kind of socks to hold down excessive foot moisture. You have all your protective gear—helmet, wrist guards, knee and elbow pads. Now you're set to go.

The first thing you'll notice is the great ankle stability you have with a first-class in-line skate. It's easy to stand up straight on the skates without much ankle wobble. That's step one. The next step is to find a flat surface that is not really fast. A grass lawn or even a carpeted room is a fine place to start. The

DUCK WALK

BASIC POSITION

first motion on an in-line skate sounds so strange that maybe it better come from an expert.

"Point your toes outward and duck walk," said Bruce Jackson of Team Rollerblade. "That's the absolute best way to start. Just duck walk in a straight line."

No, bladers don't always duck walk. The duck walk is just a way to get used to being up on your skates and moving forward. Also, by duck walking, you can get used to putting your weight on one foot, then other. In addition to that, by pointing the toes outward you have your blades in the push-off position which will soon get you rolling forward.

Continue the duck walk motion until you begin feeling more comfortable with it. Then pick up some speed, but go only fast enough so you can still keep your feet and toes pointed outward. Once you feel yourself becoming comfortable with the duck walk you may automatically find yourself falling into a natural skating position. If not, listen to Bruce Jackson.

"Keep your knees bent, weight forward and relax your upper body."

Now you're ready to start the basic stroking. Keep your hands low and in front of you, knees slightly bent and your weight still forward. Straighten your skates from the duck walk. Then point just one skate outward, and instead of duck walking, push out with that skate to the side and slightly back as you shift your weight to the forward leg.

You should feel the inside of the blade make contact with the surface and begin to push it. All the wheels on the skate should be in contact with the surface. As you push back, you should begin to roll on the forward skate. As you begin to roll, bring the pushing foot back under you, pointing it in the direction you want to go. Then transfer your weight to it.

At the same time you are transferring your weight, push out and back with the opposite leg. This second stroke should continue to propel you forward. Continue to change legs, bringing the pushing leg under you, transferring your weight, then pushing again with the other leg. Use your arms and hands for balance, keep leaning forward and keep your knees bent.

Caught in mid-stride, Darren Andrews pushes off his left foot and shows textbook balance from his right foot.
©SHAWN K. FREDERICK/NIKON

Racing.
©CANSTAR SPORTS U.S.A.

Chris Edwards shows poise and control in a textbook aerial.
©SHAWN K. FREDERICK/NIKON

Drafting and racing stride. ©CANSTAR SPORTS U.S.A.

Drafting.
©CANSTAR SPORTS U.S.A.

Ski training.
©CANSTAR SPORTS U.S.A.

One of San Diego's "radical-est" in-line
skaters, Darren Andrews, launches over the
hand rails at a nearby shopping center.
©SHAWN K. FREDERICK/NIKON

Top, left: Chris Edwards in action, showing poise and extreme control at six feet above the demo ramp.
©SHAWN K. FREDERICK/NIKON

Top, right: Chris Edwards, one of Team Rollerblade®'s finest riders, caught in mid-air in the blue skies of California.
©SHAWN K. FREDERICK/NIKON

Above: Forward flip.
©SHAWN K. FREDERICK/NIKON

Left: For Team Rollerblade®, Chris Edwards electrifies the crowd at a Bear Mountain, California demo with a back flip.
©SHAWN K. FREDERICK/NIKON

The goalie tries to make the save. ©SHAWN K. FREDERICK/NIKON

Wrist flip by forward wing player, no score! ©SHAWN K. FREDERICK/NIKON

Rushing the goalie. ©SHAWN K. FREDERICK/NIKON

Top and bottom: Goalie blocks the shot. ©SHAWN K. FREDERICK/NIKON

Guess what? You're skating.

Make sure that your first efforts at stroking are on a smooth, flat surface. If you start your duckwalk on grass or even on a carpet, you can now move to a smooth, paved surface to work on your stroking. Remember, don't get carried away and go too fast because you still don't know how to stop. That comes next. As you continue to push one foot out, then the other, concentrate on the things you are doing.

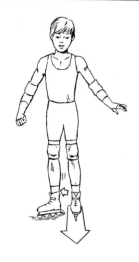

For example, make sure your weight is concentrated over the ball of your foot. You do this by keeping the knees bent and by leaning slightly forward. Try standing straight up and you will feel the difference. There is less control, less stability. You will feel much more secure on your skates the first way. With the secure feeling, you can slowly begin taking fuller strokes and swinging your arms in a rhythmic cadence with your legs.

Once again, remember these rules for basic stroking.

1. Keep your knees bent and lean forward so that your weight is concentrated over the balls of your feet.
2. Always shift your weight to your forward leg, the one that isn't pushing.
3. Move the pushing leg outward in more of a sideward motion. It will move back automatically.
4. Make sure all the wheels of your skate are in contact with the surface as you push.
5. When you bring your back foot forward again, point it in the direction you want to go.

STOPPING

If you don't learn this lesson well, you shouldn't be out on a pair of in-line skates. Because if you can't stop well chances are you will get hurt sooner or later, probably sooner. There are several ways to stop when you're blading along, the most basic way being with the brake provided with your skates. As mentioned earlier, Bruce Jackson called the brake that comes on the skates pure "gold," adding, "The brake is fantastic, the most

STRIDE

unbelievable tool on the skate. There are so many things you can do with the brake, yet a lot of people try to find other ways of stopping."

There are other ways, but not for beginners. That's why Jackson is so adamant about skaters learning to use the brake. The people who often have trouble with it are those who have crossed over from other sports.

"Many people who come over from traditional rollerskating are so familiar with the toe brake on roller skates that they have a hard time adjusting to the heel brake on an in-line skate," Jackson explains. "Even after they're blading they automatically go to a toe brake which isn't there and wind up falling on their face."

Jill Schultz, who came to in-line from an ice-skating background, acknowledges the importance of the heel brake, then admits she rarely uses it.

"The only time I actually use the heel brake is when I demonstrate it to other people," she said. "For most ice skaters, like myself, it's unnatural to go to the heel brake. I tend to use the power stop or the T-stop."

All three techniques of stopping will be discussed here. Beginners should use the heel brake before moving on to the other, more advanced techniques of stopping. The important thing, of course, is that you can stop. Whether you are just learning to stroke or have advanced to stunts, racing and hills, stopping is just as important as starting . . . maybe even more important.

THE HEEL BRAKE

Some in-line skate models have a heel brake on each skate. But these are mostly beginner models for youngsters. Most of the others have the brake on just one skate, usually the right.

"Most people tend to use their right foot to stop," explains Jill Schultz. "However, you can remove the brake and put it on the left skate if you feel more comfortable that way. It's most like being right or left-handed. You'll pick one foot and that's the foot you'll always use."

Learning the technique of the heel brake is one thing; getting adept at using it is another. Beginners may understand the principal of using the brake, but they should practice and become quite good at it before trying hills or skating at high speeds.

"A lot of people will explain the heel brake to a beginner, then give them a quick lesson on how to use it," said Jill Schultz. "But they don't go past that and tell them that they really have to practice before you head down a hill and think you'll be able to stop with no problems. You've really got to have the feel of the skate and brake, and how to apply it before taking any chances. And even then, you should also learn the other stopping options just in case. The more you know, the better control you have and the safer skater you'll be."

Okay, let's get to the basics of stopping with the heel brake. As mentioned earlier, it's something that you must do immediately after you learn the basic stroke and begin moving forward. Find a flat area where you can stroke at a slow to moderate pace. Sometimes it's a good idea to skate alongside a grass area so if you have trouble stopping you can slowly move onto the grass and coast to a stop.

The basic heel stop with the brake on the right skate is done this way. As you are gliding slowly forward either put your right foot in front of your left, or scissor your left foot back and your right foot forward at the same time. Whichever feels more comfortable. Then tilt your right foot up at the toe until the heel brake makes contact with the skating surface. Now exert pressure with your right foot. This can be helped by bending the left knee. The more pressure you put on the brake, the easier you'll stop.

That is the basic maneuver. However, the faster you're moving, the more adept you have to be to get your legs into the stopping position, bend your knee and put pressure on the brake. A beginner can quickly lose his balance at a higher speed and that's why the braking maneuver takes a lot of practice. If, for some reason, you feel you want a brake on your other skate,

2. BASIC HEEL STOP

you can simply purchase one and have it mounted on the skate. That way, you can stop with either foot.

Even after you became an accomplished skater, you'll still want to use that brake. Bruce Jackson says the heel brake is the best way to stop, even when speeding down a hill.

"Skaters love to take downhills because you get an unbelievable rush," Jackson said. "A lot of skaters really build up the speed, yet if they hit that brake they stop, maybe in 15 seconds, even at top speed."

OTHER STOPS

As mentioned before, beginners should learn to use the heel brake immediately. If you start, you must be able to stop. But once you have mastered the technique of the heel brake, it isn't a bad idea to learn the others stops as well. The second most common way of stopping on in-line skates is called the T-stop.

The principle of the T-stop is relatively simple. You bring

3. T-STOP POSITION

one skate behind you, turn your foot outward so that the trailing skate forms the top of a "T" with the straight skate, then drag the inside of the wheels on the surface to bring you to a halt. The maneuver should be done with the knees bent so that you can exert pressure with the trailing skate.

You should make sure that all the wheels of the trailing skate are dragging to equalize the pressure for maximum stopping power. Oh, yes, the toughness of your skate's wheels allow you to you use the T-stop without causing any excessive wear

4. POWER STOP

to them. Jill Schultz, for one, feels the T-stop is a very effective method of stopping.

"If you can master this stop it is equally as proficient as using the heel brake," she said. "There are times when you can combine the T-stop with some slalom turns and it will slow and stop you faster than just using the heel brake in a straight line."

Again, practice makes perfect. Start slowly and then increase your speed, using the T-stop every step of the way.

The third method of stopping is the power stop. This is a stop that has been brought to in-line skating by ice skaters. That's why Jill Schultz has said that the power stop "can be quicker than the heel brake, but a power stop can only be performed by an advanced skater."

Again, the basic technique is quite simple, yet it may take a skater some time to master it. And if he's not careful in learning the power stop, he may easily turn an ankle. To make the stop, the skater will turn his body to either the right of left. He will then thrust his lead leg out in front of him keeping the knee straight. The front foot is pushed down on the surface at a sharp angle, the contact point being the inside of the wheels.

It is the pressure of the inside of the wheels on the surface that will stop the skater. If the foot is not placed at a sharp enough angle, the skater may find his ankle bending over and he may actually fall over his front foot So this maneuver takes precise balance and a lot of practice.

The power stop is often used by roller hockey players who must start and stop quickly, changing direction very often during a shift. Most good hockey players can make the power stop using either leg as the lead leg. That way, they can always keep facing the action when they stop.

TURNING

Once you learn to skate forward and stop, the next logical step is turning. Obviously, you can't skate in a straight line forever. There are two types of turns which all in-line skaters should learn. One is a simple, glide turn, the other the more complex but faster crossover turn.

The basic turn is very similar to turning on skis. It depends on balance and the ability to lean into the turn on the proper angle. You're actually turning by riding the edges of your wheel, the outside edge of one skate; the inside edge of the other.

To turn left, your weight will be on the inside edge of your

5. LEFT TURN

right foot. Bend your knee more than normal, transfer your weight to the right and lean in the direction of the turn. Your left skate will follow suit and turn onto the outside edge. Also point your hands and knees in the direction of the turn. The more you bend the knee and the more force you can put on the inside edge of the outside foot, the better you will turn.

A right turn is just the opposite. The weight is on the inside edge of the left foot. Otherwise, the technique is exactly the

6. RIGHT TURN

same. The more you practice, the more you'll get used to the lean and the angle, and the better your balance will be. Before long, this turn will be second nature to you. But practice it both ways so you can easily turn in either direction.

The crossover turn is identical to the crossover turn on ice skates. A good skater can continue to stroke while using the crossover and actually pick up speed in the turn if she wants to.

7. CROSSOVER TURN

The basic crossover maneuver involves stepping over or across one foot with the other. The rear foot completes the motion by pushing off with the outside of the blade (as opposed to the inside with straight stroking).

Once again it is important to shift your weight at the proper time and to achieve good balance while leaning into the turn. Most skaters find it more comfortable making a right-to-left crossover. This is fine to start. But don't forget to also practice the left-to-right crossover. It might not feel as comfortable, but it is important to be able to turn both ways.

To make a right-to-left crossover turn, begin leaning to the left and shifting your weight to the outside edge of the left skate. With all your weight on your left leg, lift your right leg and bring the skate over the top off the left, bringing it back to the surface pointing in the direction of the turn and slightly on the inside edge of the wheels.

At the same time the right skate is placed down, push away from the right leg with the left, using the outside edge of the blade for the push. This stroke will keep you up to speed or even increase it when you accomplish the maneuver. After completing the push, bring the left leg back to the starting position opposite the right and cross over once again.

As always, keep your knees bent and lean forward into the turn. You will also learn to keep you hands in front of you and to eventually swing them into the turn as well. Once you have perfected the right-to-left turn, then start working on the left-to-right turn, just reversing the leg movements and using the left leg to make the crossover.

"Turning is actually easier than stopping," said Jill Schultz. "It's just a matter of weight distribution and getting used to using your inside and outside edges. It should be practiced in a large, flat area. The crossover is exactly the same as on ice skates and if you come over from ice skating and begin doing crossover and smooth stroking, you can almost forget you're blading and think you're out on the ice."

Jill also said the crossover turn on in-line skates is easier than with conventional roller skates.

"You have more maneuverability and speed to begin with,"

she said. "The boot is lighter weight; the ankle support better. When you do a crossover turn on a roller skate the four wheels and wider flat surface cause the foot to stay flat and the skater to bend from the ankle to get the lean. On an in-line skate, you just lean all the way from the bottom of your foot to the hip.

"That's one reason I think the in-line skate is a safer piece of equipment than a roller skate. On a roller skate you're sitting up higher and the wheel base is shorter, so you have that falling forwards and backwards feeling more. And with an in-line skate after awhile it almost seems as if you don't even have a skate on at all."

Turning is another skill that must be learned as part of your basic course in blading. Once you can stroke, stop and turn you can go out and enjoy the sport. As you skate and practice you'll become more comfortable on your skates and your skills will improve. You'll begin to feel that you want to do more and more. Now you're ready to learn additional skills and maneuvers.

SKATING BACKWARD

Skating backward on in-line skates is again very similar to doing the same thing on ice skates. Someone crossing over from ice skating to blading can pick up this skill almost instantly. For those who have started blading from the beginning, it may take a little longer. But learning to skate backward is not really difficult.

However, you do not simply reverse the movements of forward stroking. To skate backward, you have to create a very smooth action of the skates, both feet working together, with the blades remaining in contact with the skating surface. To begin, stand on a flat surface with your feet positioned directly under your shoulders. As always, bend slightly at the knees.

Step one is to turn the toes of both skates inward, pigeon style, and at the same time bring your knees together. You will be pushing off the inside edge of both blades. Unlike forward stroking, both feet will perform the stroke at the same time.

Start by pushing outward with both feet, keeping your weight on the inside edges of the blades.

Continue to push until your feet are both outside your shoulders. By then you'll begin to move backwards. With the inside edge of the blades continuing to contact the surface, bring each foot back to the starting position in a crisp arc, almost making the stroke appear like a question mark and reversed question mark. Once your feet are back at the starting position, still pigeon-toed, simply repeat the stroke. With a little practice you'll begin to smooth out and pick up speed.

You can turn by shifting your weight to one leg or the other and simply pushing harder with the opposite leg. But the best way to turn while skating backwards is to use the crossover stroke. This takes some real practice shifting your weight, keeping your balance and coordinating the stroke.

First you have to be good enough to skate backwards at a moderate speed. If you want to cross over to the left you must shift the weight on your left foot to the outside edge of the blade. At the same time you are pushing back with the outside edge of the left skate, slide your right skate across the left. Then push out with the inside blade of the right foot and bring your left foot back to the start position. You then shift the weight back to the outside edge of the left skate, push and cross over again.

BACKWARD

You should be pushing outward at an angle that will keep you moving backwards around the curve and your skates should stay as close to the skating surface as possible. To cross over to the right, just reverse the procedure, beginning by putting the weight on the outside edge of the right blade and sliding your left skate across the right.

This may sound complex and difficult. The best way to learn is to watch a good skater perform the maneuver and then imitate him. It's always easier to watch someone who is proficient in sport do the things you want to try. That will make these kinds of instructions even more clear.

Once you can skate backwards and cross over smoothly, you can learn to go from skating forwards to backwards, and back again. This involves a pivot-type move on one skate that will help you to swing your body around. With a move like this, it's almost essential to watch someone do it. If you are already a confident basic skater, you should pick it up quickly.

Now you have the basics of blading. Once you step on your skates and practice all the moves outlined in this chapter, you'll be able to thoroughly enjoy your new life as a blader. When you're out there, you'll undoubtedly meet other bladers, some of whom are into stunts, racing and even rollerhockey. If you want to join in on the excitement, keep practicing the basics. Then you'll soon be ready to cross the line to more advanced techniques. And, as always remember rule number one. Skate smart; skate safe.

PART FOUR

ADVANCED SKATING

STUNTS AND STREET STYLES

To enter the world of stunt and street-style skating, you must already have the basics. Listen to the advice of Jill Schultz of Team Rollerblade.

"Once you feel comfortable where you can stop, you can skate both forwards and backwards, turn from frontward to backward and back again, and do your crossovers in both directions, then you're ready to go on and learn something new and exciting.

"To begin doing more complex stunts and maneuvers, it's best to skate with someone who is already experienced in these areas. It doesn't necessarily have to be a fully certified instructor, but at least someone who is already proficient in the stunt you want to try. Using that approach will help you learn how to do it more quickly and safely. In other words, it's best to watch someone perform the stunt first."

Bruce Jackson, also a senior member of Team Rollerblade, knows how great the lure of the sport can become, especially to youngsters with a desire to try new things. He sounds a warning to those who want to jump into more advanced skating.

"As I said before, your average in-line skater really tends to want to push it," Jackson says. "That's the one thing about an in-line skater. It's so much fun you just want to do more and more and more of it. With some people, it becomes almost a macho type of thing. They just want to go out there and take off."

So the byword is to avoid trying too much too soon, and to work with an experienced skater with every new thing you do. The following will give you the basics, the way that you do some of the more popular forms of advanced skating. Learn it slowly and don't rush.

JUMPING

The ability to jump on in-line skates is basic to almost all forms of advanced skating and stunts. It's an absolute must to feel comfortable with your jumps before you move on to other things. Begin conservatively and build up your ability slowly. In fact, the first thing you jump can be simply a chalk line on the street or a crack in the sidewalk, nothing that can trip you up and cause a bad fall.

There are two things to keep in mind right away. One is that you always must have enough speed to make a jump. Speed increases momentum. In other words, the more speed the higher or farther you can go.

Also, when you are preparing to jump, don't just worry about getting your feet over the barrier. Rather think in terms of getting your entire body over. That way, you'll concentrate on propelling your entire body into the air, not only your feet. By doing this, it eliminates a tendency for the jumper to look down at his feet. He should continue to look straight ahead before and during his jump.

Most times, a jumper should get ready to jump about five feet before the obstacle. The best way to take off is with both feet at the same time. Some bladers like to push off with their stronger leg, but they get less stability and ultimately less lift this way.

As you approach the jump, glide into the takeoff point with both feet together. Bend even more at the knees and lean forward. Your arms should be out in front. Just before taking off, drop your arms and then throw them upward and straighten your knees. Once off the ground, bring your knees up toward your chest to give your legs more height.

When you land, be sure to put one foot about a skate's length in front of the other, much like a ski jumper does. This allows you to have a longer and more stable landing base. Most jumpers like to land with their stronger foot coming down just ahead of the other. You'll instinctively know which is the stronger. It's like being right-handed or left-handed.

Also be ready to stride forward as soon as you hit. This, too, will give you more stability on the landing, just in case it isn't perfect. Some advanced skaters will land and glide, but this takes practice. With practice, you can begin jumping higher and higher objects. Remember also to use objects that "give," such as a cardboard box. If you're jumping a solid object, like a fence or railing, and you miss, the chance of serious injury is much greater.

Once you begin to become a good jumper, you might try grabbing your boots in midair. This is a more showy move and can also give you more height. It can also keep your body in a tighter tuck and give you more control when you prepare to land.

CURB AND RAMP JUMPING

Curb jumping is a slight variation of the regular jump. By using the same jumping technique described above and launching yourself off a curb, you will automatically get the feeling of more height and you will go farther. If you're going off an eight-inch-high curb, for example, you will start your

JUMP

8.

9.

10.

(PHOTOS 8–10)
BASIC CURB JUMP

aerial act eight inches higher than if you were jumping off a flat surface. But remember, you'll be coming down a long way, too, so remember to concentrate on that landing.

By practicing curb jumping the blader is actually starting to train for the next logical step, jumping off a ramp. In a sense, jumping off a ramp is something like a ski jump or a ramp jump on water skis. Judge your speed by the distance you want to go. More speed, more distance, because the ramp is going to help launch your body.

Get into your stride and speed as you approach the ramp. About 10 feet or so before hitting the ramp stop stroking and go into a glide. As you do, dip down into almost a deep knee bend, your body tucked tight, arms bent and drawn back at the shoulder. The natural tendency when you first hit a ramp is to bring your weight back onto your heels. This is wrong. Lean forward enough to keep your weight on the balls of your feet.

Right before you hit the top spring out from your knees and also with your arms. Try to keep your body slightly forward in the air. If you lean back you might not be able to recover in time to land properly. As soon as you take off, you've got to concentrate on that landing, which is similar again to a ski jumper.

As with the basic jump, you should land with one foot a

skate's length in front of the other. But because you are coming down from greater height, you must cushion the landing by bending your knees. Then, at the moment of impact, bend them even more, almost to the point of going into a deep knee bend position. When you start to glide, straighten up immediately and begin to stride.

Ramp jumping is exciting and thrilling. You'll get that blader's "rush" when you become good enough to go for it. But get there gradually. Start slowly and become a good surface and curb jumper before taking to the ramps.

STAIR RIDING

Stair riding is yet another form of jumping. Or perhaps it's better to say that it is a series of quick landings, one after another. In essence, you are skating down a flight of stairs without losing speed and slowing to a halt. But you've got to stay in complete control so you don't end up gaining speed and wiping out.

The obvious way to practice this is to first try it on stairs that have a hand rail which you can hold onto. You should start down the stairs with your feet maybe six inches apart, one in front of the other. It is the same kind of foot position you would use landing on a jump. The front foot should be your stronger foot, which will give you more stability to absorb the jarring as you descend the stairs.

Balance is also important. Keep your knees bent with your hands in front and your weight slightly in front of you. Don't lean too far forward, however, as that could cause too much of a buildup of momentum. Another way to keep control when riding stairs is to keep your weight toward the back of the skates, near the heel. That's because the toes of the skate lose contact with the surface of the stairs as you descend.

Also be sure to keep the wheels of the skates pointed straight ahead. Then simply continue to lead with the stronger foot and bounce down. Start slowly, with two or three stairs and holding to the rail. Don't begin with a real steep stair, either. Try to

11.

12.

13.

14.

(PHOTOS 11–14) STAIR RIDING

start with wide steps that aren't steep and as you get better you can try longer and steeper staircases.

Stair riding is definitely a showy street maneuver. Just be smart about it. Never try riding stairs on a dare if you haven't done it before. And don't do it simply because you're playing follow the leader. The leader may be a much more accomplished skater than you. Be smart and skate smart.

TAKING HILLS

All skaters want to take hills sooner or later, some just for the exercise of going up, others for the thrill of going down. There are different techniques for each. Uphill climbing is a matter of strength and endurance, as well as a slightly different stroking method.

Many new skaters make the mistake of attacking a hill, trying to blast up it with long, full strokes. This is simply the wrong way to do it. Going uphill, you aren't going to get the same long glide that a full stroke will produce on a flat surface. The correct way is to take the hill with strong, but short strokes.

An uphill climb is also one of the few times a blader doesn't bend much at the waist. He should keep his back much straight, and try to keep his weight right over the balls of his feet. If the weight is too far front or too far to the back of the foot he will lose leverage and power.

Uphill climbing is a challenge and also an aerobic training tool if the skater is looking for a great workout or maybe even getting in shape to race. The technique always stays the same and the short strokes should be rhythmic and steady. Make it a goal not to slow down as you near the top.

Going downhill the emphasis has to be on control. Lose control on a steep hill and you may take a ride you didn't expect. In other words, unless you know how to control your skates, change direction, slow down and/or stop, a downhill ride can lead to a serious injury.

Like a downhill skier, a good downhill blader will get into a tight tuck position, knees bent, feet close together with one slightly in front of the other, hands in close at the side. He will keep his weight forward and on the balls of his feet. In the tuck position, the head is also held down, but not so far that it will keep the blader from looking straight ahead.

Don't ever stand up straight while skating downhill. This will result in immediate loss of control. Also, make sure you are an expert at using your heel brake. Even traveling at top speed, a good braker will be able to stop within 15 or so seconds. In addition, there several other maneuvers that will slow you down or allow you to stop if you sense danger during your downhill run.

To slow down without using the heel brake, a blader can also use the T-stop, dragging the foot just enough to slow momentum. A couple of quick, slalom-like turns will also slow the pace. You can use the turning technique learned earlier, but be sure you can make the maneuver at a high speed. And a final way to stop is to continue the turn until you are skating sideways on the hill or even start back up it a bit.

A final word of caution. Before you attempt to skate down any hill, check for potential hazards. That includes traffic, deep ruts in the surface, pedestrians or even animals. Any one of the above that cause bladers a problem and make a great downhill run a bummer.

RAMP STUNTS

Jumping is not the only reason bladers love ramps. Ramps have become the same kind of challenge to bladers that they have been to skateboarders and BMX bikers. This is where a tal-

(PHOTOS 16–18)
HOW TO SLOW DOWN ON DOWNHILL RIDE— DOWNHILL SLALOM TURN STOP

16.

17.

18.

ented blader can really strut his stuff. But the tricks and stunts are difficult, take a lot of practice, and can be dangerous. Ramps are not for beginners or the tender at heart. You must be skilled and confident before you tackle these advanced maneuvers.

Launch ramps for jumping have already been discussed. The other two main types of ramps are quarter-pipe and half-pipe. The quarter-pipe is a one-section ramp with a single peak and single valley. In other words, you can go up and down. The half-pipe had peaks on both sides and a valley in between. You can go up one side, come back down and then go up the other side, and you can do it over and over again.

Before you start any kind of ramp work remember this. Protective equipment is essential. Be sure to wear a helmet, knee, elbow and wrist pads. This will help you to avoid scrapes, bruises and bumps of all kinds. The importance of the helmet, of course, speaks for itself.

The numbers of moves and stunts that can be done on the ramps is endless, too many to include here. In fact, hotdogging bladers with a lot of skills can improvise and invent new stunts as they go along. Rather than try to instruct beginners or even intermediate skaters in the many intricacies of ramp riding, we will instead just give you the basic techniques of going up and down the ramps. To become more involved with this part of blading, it is best to work with a qualified instructor, an experienced skater or to even attend an in-line skating camp.

To do any kind of ramp riding you have to know how to go up the ramp, turn and come back down again. This is called gyrating or pumping the ramp. Begin by approaching the ramp with a smooth stride and gather enough speed to take you quickly up the ramp. The area just before the ramp turns upward is called the transitional area. At this point bend your knees, lower your arms and relax your legs. This will put you into a full glide.

As you start up the ramp you should have the feeling that your weight is in your upper body, not your legs. When you approach the top of the ramp slowly straighten your legs and

QUARTERPIPE

back. The trick here is to time your pivot at almost the same point the upward swing of the ramp will stop you. It should happen almost at the top.

Decide ahead of time in which direction you prefer to turn. If you are going to turn right, you would drop your right arm and shoulder, while at the same time raising your left arm and shoulder. Let your arms lead your upper torso into the turn. At

20. GRABBING RAMP WITH TWO HANDS

the same time simply pivot your skates in the direction of the turn. Don't try to jump into the turn or push off the ramp in any way. If you do this, you might find yourself in the air and headed for a wipeout.

By just pivoting your feet the natural momentum of your body and the position you are in at the top of the ramp will take care of the rest and you should find yourself in position to skate down. As you start down, just bend your knees and bend forward again at the waist. If you come back down straight you may find yourself falling backwards as soon as you reach the bottom.

Remember also to put one foot about a skate's length in front of the other as you descend. This position is similar to landing on a jump. It will give you more stability and also help you gain speed if you are going to go up the other side of a half-pipe. If you are working on a quarter-pipe, of course, the descent is the end of the stunt.

Advanced stunt skaters can do a number of things on the ramp. Some will reach over and touch the top of the ramp with one hand as they pivot and push off. Others will find still other ways to make the pivot stand out, acrobatic moves that often take them into mid-air, something definitely not for everyone. A few others can even grab the top of the ramp with both hands and do a complete handstand before returning to the ramp and skating down. It takes a skater with good gymnastic ability to do this. Don't try it unless you can do a similar handstand without your skates. Done by an inexperienced skater without gymnastic training, this can be a dangerous move.

In fact, the more stunts and difficult moves you try on your blades, the more danger. That's why it is important to work with an instructor or a very experienced skater who has the patience to teach you. And it always helps to watch others perform the stunts before you try them. If you are afraid to try something or feel you don't yet have the skills to do it, then wait. Keep practicing and you'll get better. In other words, once again continue to skate smart and skate safe.

PART FIVE

RACING

One of the fastest-growing aspects of in-line skating is racing. It had to happen. No matter what means man has used to propel himself over the years, each one has always lent itself to racing. Speed skating on ice has been a worldwide and Olympic sport for years. Without the restrictions of ice, racing on in-line skates has become much more versatile.

Bladers can race around the same kind of oval courses as ice skaters, but they can also go out on the open road for cross-country-type races of various distances. There are even some bladers beginning to skate over ultra-long distances. In-line skating has also taken over some former rollerskating races where the only requirement is the races be on wheels. Since in-line skates can attain more speed than conventional roller skates, the bladers have dominated.

Racing on in-line skates has also attracted many crossover athletes. Ice skaters can train using an almost identical technique and don't have to worry about finding ice time. Cross-country skiers and bicycle racers also find that competing on in-line skates not only keeps them in condition for their other sports, but is supercompetitive in itself. And runners looking to continue training, but with a much lower impact and less abuse of their legs and joints, have taken up in-line racing as an alternative and as an extra added activity.

To become involved with racing on a regular basis is serious business. It's more than turning to your friend and betting you can beat him to the end of the block or reach that distant fence faster than he can. Racing takes a real commitment as well as some serious training. No one would think of running a 10K road race or a marathon without being adequately prepared. The same goes for racing on in-line skates. You've got to learn all over again about the care of your skates, about training methods and racing strategy. But if you're competitive and want to get in great shape at the same time, racing may be the way for you to go.

THE FIVE-WHEEL SKATE

The five-wheel racing skate is the best in-line skate you can buy. Even those who don't race sometimes buy them for their overall quality. The longer frame needed to accommodate five wheels seems to give the skater a more stable ride, not to mention a faster one. Those who love to ride hills sometimes favor the five-wheel skate. The longer frame enables the skater to take a longer stride and use more power when he is stroking along.

However, as mentioned earlier, the five-wheel skate isn't for everyone and really shouldn't be used by recreational skaters and especially those who want to do tricks, dancing and even stunts. Racing and hill riding are the two areas where the five-wheel skate becomes a fantastic investment.

Five-wheelers usually come with an exceptionally high grade of bearings, the best available on the highest priced models. These bearings are generally packed with a thick grease to extend their life. This lubricant will, however, keep the skater from attaining the maximum possible speed. Serious racers will almost always alter the lubricant on the bearings.

If the bearings have removable caps they can be opened and the bearings soaked in a solvent, such as kerosene, for at least several hours. This treatment will effectively remove the heavy grease. After you clean and dry the bearings, they can then be repacked with a good grade of light oil so they can attain maximum speed. The bearings may not last as long, but they'll allow you to do your best in a race.

Should you buy a pair of skates that have sealed bearings, you can still soak them in a solvent. Enough will seep through to remove some of the original heavy grease. A second soaking with either a white lithium or silicon-based lubricant will complete the treatment and give you some additional speed.

In addition, serious racers must pay attention to the wheels on their skates. With in-line skates, a softer wheel will give more speed. The wheels are thin to begin with, and the softer wheel will flatten out just enough to give the racer more road surface under him and thus allow for a more powerful stroke.

TECHNIQUES OF RACING

The techniques of racing on in-line skates are almost identical to speed skating on ice. Ice skaters also have an extra long blade on their skates and take full advantage of it.

Unless you are in an all-out sprint, your objective should be to take as long and as powerful stroke as you can while exerting a minimum effort with your body. In other words, you don't want to burn out too quickly.

First, you must keep your weight forward at all times, bending at the waist even more so than with a regular stroke. This not only keeps your momentum where it belongs, but cuts down on wind resistance. In racing, every little edge counts. The knees, of course, remain bent, and with the exception of the start and finish, the racer must try to stay as relaxed as possible.

The stroke is the same as a normal skating stroke, only it is longer and more powerful. Since the most powerful part of the stroke comes at the start, when your legs are directly under your body, make sure you take advantage of this by bringing each leg fully under your torso, so that your knees are almost touching. Then generate as much power as you can from that first 12 inches or so of thrust. Power dissipates the further you push your leg away from your body, but you still need the finishing part of the stroke for smoothness and glide.

Speed skaters should also make sure they are pushing out to the side rather than behind them. To help you do this concentrate on keeping your knees pointed straight ahead during the entire stroke. This is especially important at a point when you begin to tire. That's when there is a tendency to get sloppy and lose the rhythm of the stroke.

It is also important to move the upper body as little as possible during the stroke, especially when the skater is simply maintaining speed, not sprinting, climbing a hill or trying to pass another skater. As you have probably seen with ice skaters, this is often done by skating with both hands behind your back and on a curve with one hand behind you, only the outer hand pumping.

By putting both hands behind you, you'll also find yourself automatically in a good tuck position. Now it is just your legs and lower body doing the work so you are conserving energy. Pumping the arms does not help greatly during these portions of the race. Skating with one or both arms behind you will not feel natural at first. You may not feel you have the same kind of balance as you do when your arms are out front. But keep at it. Soon it will feel natural and you'll marvel at the energy you'll save.

When you do have to pump your arms, pump them in a straight, front-to-back arc, first one then the other in rhythm with your legs. Don't throw them out to the side. Economy of motion is one of the secrets to good racing. Wasted motion means loss of speed and you'll tire faster.

One word of caution. Skating for long periods in a tuck position can sometimes result in a sore back. This can be alleviated somewhat by doing exercises to strengthen lower back muscles and also by following a regular stretching program. But it is sometimes an occupational hazard and a condition that needs occasional rest.

Races vary in distance from short sprints to 5, 10 and 30 kilometers. But more and more skaters are looking to go longer distances, like the marathon and ultramarathon. Training methods and race strategies differ for each type of event. For the shorter races, for instance, the bladers will start by actually running off the starting line, then quickly moving into their stride and trying for the best possible position they can get within the pack. With longer races, a pace car will drive slowly in front of the racers, allowing everyone to warm up. Once it reaches the starting line, the pace car pulls away and the racers are on their own.

One of the most important skills a racer must learn is that of drafting. Runners and ice skaters will do the same thing. Drafting is simply the act of falling in close behind another racer and allowing him to break the wind for you. In other words, he is getting wind resistance, but you are skating in a kind of air pocket created by his body. So you can keep pace with him while expending less energy.

To draft properly you must stay very close to the skater in front of you and match both his stride and arm movements. This takes practice. You don't want to get so close that you risk bumping him and maybe tripping both of you up. At the same time, if you are too far behind, you won't actually be drafting at all because the distance between you will be too great and you'll be out of the air pocket. You must stay within several feet of the blader in front of you.

In road races, bladers often help each other by taking turns leading and drafting. The lead skater will often warn the racer behind him of any road hazards such as potholes and bumps. Of course, the leader may also try to break the pack and the skater behind by surging and pulling away. But these strategies often don't happen until the final portion of the race. More drafting will occur in longer races than in shorter ones.

Racers must also learn to pace themselves, to know their

own bodies well enough to be able to judge just how fast to skate during each part of the race. The strategy of pacing is the same for a blader as it is for a runner. If you go out too fast and burn yourself out during the first half of a race, you'll likely run out of gas during the crucial final part. Conversely, if you allow yourself to get too far behind during the first half, you'll have to expend too much energy catching up with the leaders and won't have enough left for the final stretch.

Most inexperienced racers like to hang back at the beginning, trying to maintain contact with the lead pack. If you can do that, you can begin to pick up the pace in the second half of the race. Ideally a skater who has paced himself well will gradually make up the distance to be in a position to win the race at crunch time, in the final stages when everyone at or near the front begins sprinting toward the finish line.

Training methods can vary from racer to racer, and also from distance to distance. Every blader who wants to race must make sure he or she is in tip-top condition before entering any kind of competition. You can race when you're in good condition and work to make your conditioning even better. But if you are in poor condition, you shouldn't race at all.

Beginners should talk to other racers or maybe even find a good running coach for training tips about getting in shape. Training must be done regularly, almost every day, with the rules of general fitness addressed earlier also applying to races. Since there is less chance of an injury for bladers than for runners because of the low-impact nature of the sport, they should be able to adhere to a regular training schedule with no problem at all.

As a general rule, those competing in shorter races should do more speed work, while those racing over longer distances must concentrate on endurance. Speed won't help over a 30-kilometer distance if you don't have the endurance to keep pace with the leaders for the entire race. And endurance won't do you much good in a 100-meter sprint which is over almost before it begins.

Seek out a coach and let him map out what he feels will be the best program for you. He will take into consideration your condition at the starting point, your ability on your skates, your speed and strength and the type of racer he feels you can be. All these factors will influence which events are best for you and how you should train.

Training methods include alternating between a series of sprints and long-distance skating, interval work where you might skate at a steady pace for a distance, then go into a sprint, then back to the original pace, then another sprint. This type of training is a great conditioner and the same program followed by runners.

Two other things to remember. No matter how long a distance you are racing continue to follow the basic procedure of warming up and cooling down. Do not stretch before a race. Warm up the same way you would for an afternoon of stop and go skating. Take a slow skate to get yourself ready, relaxing and gradually getting loose. After the race, do some of your basic stretching, just as you would after a good training session.

For those involved in longer races, remember to drink plenty of fluids, especially on a hot day. Some bladers carry their own water bottles. During a long race there might be water stations or fans offering water along the way, as they do in road races and marathons. Remember, if you don't replenish fluids during a long, hot race you could become dehydrated or suffer a heat stroke.

Racing is one of the fastest growing aspects of in-line skating. There are more sanctioned races than ever and some day there could be a regular professional circuit. Jill Schultz feels that racing is perhaps the first area where in-line skating could make the breakthrough to professionalism.

"There has been a big growth in racing already," she said. "There are race series happening all year round and they are getting a large turnout all over the country. In fact, skaters from Europe are beginning to join in, so you know it's catching on."

If you want to do more than just skate for fun, but can't play hockey and aren't the type of person to do stunts, then racing on in-line skates might be just for you.

PART SIX

LET'S PLAY ROLLERHOCKEY

No one will dispute the fact that in-line skating is growing by leaps and bounds. Although there are more converts to the sports every single day, no one area is growing faster than that of rollerhockey. The ironic part of this is that the sport was originally invented by a pair of ice hockey players who wanted to be able to practice the sport without ice. Now there are rollerhockey leagues springing up all over, with both ice hockey players and newcomers joining in the action and the fun. And no one seems to miss the ice at all.

Rollerhockey itself is not a new sport. Kids have been playing it on city playgrounds and on makeshift rinks for years. Only they played it on rollerskates, sometimes using a rubber ball as a "puck" and even using broomsticks instead of hockey sticks. In other words, they played with whatever tools were available and it wasn't very organized. On in-line skates, rollerhockey is a very different game.

"It's a faster game on in-line skates, no doubt about it," said

Bruce Jackson, who has watched rollerhockey spring up all over his native southern California. "You can turn a lot quicker and handle the puck a lot smoother on blades than on conventional roller skates. You just have all that added maneuverability of an in-line skate."

While many of the elements of ice hockey remain, rollerhockey is a different game in a number of significant ways. First of all, there is very little violent physical contact. The hard, slambang checking of ice hockey is not permitted. That's just one way rollerhockey on in-line skates is a faster game, depending more on the individual skating, passing and shooting skills of the players.

Secondly, it is played with five players on a team instead of six. There are only two forwards (as opposed to three in ice hockey), two defensemen and a goaltender on each team. This also makes for a more wide open, free-skating game. In addition, there is no offsides rule which, in ice hockey, keeps all the offensive players confined to one part of the rink and doesn't allow any player to precede the puck into enemy territory. In rollerhockey, players are free to roam the rink without worrying about where the puck is.

The result is a game packed with fast, stop-and-go skating, very few pauses in the action and a constant flow of end-to-end rushes, exciting passes and a large number of breakaways. Because the faster pace of rollerhockey can really wear out the participants, each game consists of two 15-minute halves as opposed to three 20-minute periods in ice hockey.

This is a highly competitive sport that takes a great deal of speed, quickness and skill to play. It tends to be a high-scoring, crowd-pleasing game where size and strength isn't nearly as important as skating ability, puck handling and elusiveness. Let's take a closer look.

SPECIAL EQUIPMENT

As you have already undoubtedly figured out, rollerhockey is not ice hockey and if you play ice hockey you can't just put on the same gear and throw on your skates. Since the emphasis is on speed rather than hitting, the equipment used by the skaters is ultralight so it will barely hinder their movement nor cause any excessive fatigue.

Helmets are mandatory, of course, but they are made of a lightweight material and have a clear face shield attached. The backs of the gloves are padded and have a protective cuff to also cover the wrists. Elbow pads are also a good idea since they can protect against falls.

Many players wear sweatpants with hockey shorts pulled over them to protect the buttocks from bruises and abrasions. Both padded knee guards and shin pads are required because getting banged with an errant hockey stick can hurt. Boys and men must also wear a protective cup. Because there is no checking, the bulky shoulder pads and padded pants of the ice hockey player are not necessary.

The puck is lighter than an ice hockey puck, but it is made from a hard, synthetic material and when flying through the air at top speed can be dangerous. Therefore, the goaltender must be extra well protected. He must wear a cage-style mask, a chest protector, protective cup and lightweight leg pads. Like ice hockey goalies, he will wear a glove on his free hand and also a glove to hold the stick in his other hand. The stick-side glove has a lightweight blocker attached to it. That's a rectangular pad that protects the back of the stick hand and the exposed part of the forearm almost up to the elbow.

One quick word about the skates. Most hockey players will rocker the wheels of their skates (see chapter on care and maintenance of skates) to give them more maneuverability when turning and pivoting. So if you want to play roller-hockey, make sure the skates you buy have the option to have the wheels rockered.

SKATING, STICKHANDLING, PASSING AND SHOOTING

You've got to already be an accomplished skater if you decide to play rollerhockey. In other words, you've got to be able to skate both forward and backward, turn in either direction, cross over going both forward and backward, be able to stop and start quickly, change direction and generate great speed with a quick burst of energy. If you're not comfortable doing all these things, keep practicing them before you start playing hockey. The skating part must be second nature to a roller-hockey player. He can't think about it when he's in the midst of a heated game.

That's because he has to concentrate on the game—on stick-handling, passing, shooting and defense. His skates are simply a means to allow him to do these other things and be in the right place at the right time. Now that you know what you have to do as a skater, let's take a look at the other skills new players must develop.

While skating ability is of the utmost importance to roller-hockey players, the best skaters don't necessarily make the best all-around players. The way a player uses his stick to control the puck can be just as important as how well he skates. The stick should be held with the fingers, not the palms of the hands. This way a player will have more movement and more whip with the stick when he rolls his wrists.

The top hand is held up near the end of the stick nearly all the time, while the bottom hand moves around. It is held up higher when a player is carrying or dribbling the puck. It slides down lower on the shaft when the player prepares to launch a slap shot. For a right-handed player, the right hand is the lower hand. The left-hander does it just the opposite.

The lower hand is always the power hand, both for passing and shooting. That's why the player will often move it up and down the shaft.

When handling the puck, a player must always keep his head up. If you have to watch the puck to keep it on your stick, you won't be able to watch your teammates or your opponents. And you won't play the game very well. There are two basic ways to carry the puck, the side-to-side and front-to-back methods.

In the side-to-side method, the skater moves the puck one way, then crosses his stick over it, catches it on his blade and moves it back the other way. He keeps repeating this movement as he works his way up the rink. In the front-to-back method, the player pushes the puck out ahead of him, then reaches out with his stick to control it before pushing it ahead again. With both methods, the player should always try to maintain control with the middle of the blade of the stick.

Carrying the puck either way is simply a matter of practice. You've got to get the feel of the puck on your stick so you don't have to watch it. Like so many other skills, start slowly, skating at a very slow pace while you are working the puck back and forth. Pretty soon you'll be picking up speed and continuing to control the puck.

Once a skater has the basics of carrying, he can begin practicing control of the puck while he makes sharp turns and crossovers. He must learn to keep it on the blade of his stick while he makes the sharp move, then he can begin dribbling it once again. He should even be able to control it while making a complete, 180-degree pivot.

After awhile, a stickhandler will learn to fake, pretending to move the puck and his body one way, then suddenly going the other. Fakes are very important in getting around defenders. If a defender reaches for the puck with his stick, the attacking player has got to pull it away quickly and still control it.

The more quickness you have while skating and stickhandling, the better you will be. Sometimes you have to throw the puck quickly out to the side, then make your move to recapture it before the defensive player can. A good coach will be able to show you a variety of "moves" that will help you with your stickhandling even more. It might even be wise to practice carrying the puck with just one hand on the stick. Sometimes a player might use his body and free arm to help him through a tight spot.

One thing to remember about stickhandling. Don't overdo it. Don't try to be a one-man gang and rush the puck through the defense to the goal. Sometimes the situation calls for a pass. And if you are so intent on stickhandling that you don't see an open teammate, you can hurt your team.

*   *   *

Passing is another important skill each rollerhockey player must have. Since this is a more wide-open game than ice hockey, players must learn to make quick, accurate passes. And they must often be able to pass the puck a long distance. Every player must be ready to both make and receive a pass. And since both the passer and receiver are often moving at top speed, a good passer must be able to put the puck in the spot where his teammate will be when the puck arrives, not where his teammate is when he makes the pass. You must have anticipation and lead the pass receiver.

A good hockey player can pass from both his forehand and backhand sides and can receive a pass the both ways. When passing, the puck should be pushed across the surface of the rink. It should not be slapped or golfed, which could make the puck leave the playing surface.

21. FORWARD HAND

There are a number of passes that each player should practice. The most popular is the forehand pass where the passer simply keeps his stick low to the playing surface and slides the puck to a teammate. Be sure to maintain surface contact with your stick. If you lift your stick as you make the pass, you might lift the puck, as well. The backhand pass is made the same way, except that the puck is coming off the outside of the blade. The right side of the stick is the backhand side for a right-handed skater.

Another popular pass is the drop pass. This can often catch the defense napping if it is done quickly. In a sense, this is really not a pass. The passer is simply leaving the puck for a teammate skating behind him. It is done as a skater moves quickly up the rink, the defense guarding him closely. He should be using the front-to-back method of carrying the puck and when the puck gets to the front he just leaves it and skates ahead at full speed. His teammate coming in behind him can pick the puck up and hopefully work for a shot on goal.

23. BACK PASS

A player must also be able to occasionally make a back pass. This pass is almost always made by the backhand part of the stick. The player who is skating forward controls the puck on the outside of the blade and passes with a backward stroke to a teammate behind him. Once again anticipation is important. If a back pass is made near the goal, a teammate swooping in on the puck can often get an immediate clear shot.

When receiving passes, players should always hold their stick loosely in their hands. This is the equivalent of having "soft hands" when catching a football. In other words, the puck will nestle onto the blade of the stick. The player can also help more by cupping his stick, or laying the blade at an angle over the incoming puck. Just be careful not to lift the stick off the playing surface. If you hold the stick too tightly, the incoming puck may bounce away, giving the defense a chance to get it.

Accurate shooting is another important part of rollerhockey. In fact, because a rollerhockey goal is smaller than an ice hockey goal, accuracy is extremely important. The ice hockey net is 4 feet high and 6 feet wide. In rollerhockey, the net is 3½ feet high and just 5 feet wide. The technique of shooting, however, is the same in each sport.

There are two basic shots in hockey—the wrist shot and the slap shot. The slap shot is the harder of the two, but not as easy to control. The most important part of shooting is balance. For maximum power, the shooter must fire away with his weight on the lead or front foot. This means the left foot for a right-handed shooter and the right foot for a southpaw. The upper hand on the stick guides the shot, while the lower provides the power.

The wrist shot can be taken at any time and usually from any place in the attacking zone. When taking a wrist shot, always start with the puck as close to the heel of the blade as possible. The right-handed shooter will snap his left or top wrist back while the right or bottom hand snaps the stick forward. With the puck back near the heel of the blade the shooter will generate more power. Hand positions for the left-handed shooter are simply reversed.

As he snaps both wrists, the shooter should shift his weight from the rear to the front skate. He must also be sure to follow through with his motion, even after the puck has left the stick. Follow through directly at the spot in the goal where you have aimed your shot.

With practice, a player can control the height of a wrist shot. He can simply keep it on the playing surface or make it rise up and go through the air. To get the puck to wrist, the shooter must cup the blade over the puck. The wrist snap will then give it lift. If a shot is too high, however, it will go over the top of the goal. It takes a lot of practice to control the direction and height of a shot.

Someone once said that a good slap shooter is like a home run hitter in baseball. It is a booming, hard shot that isn't always so easy to control. But if it is on goal, it is a difficult shot for the goaltender to stop. When shooting the slap shot, the shooter will be taking a full swing at the puck.

He does this with his feet facing the goal and the puck beside him. The shooter then begins by raising his stick until it is at least waist high. Some will raise it even more. The stick should hit the surface just behind the puck. As the shooter shifts his weight from back to front, the rear foot will sometimes come up off the surface. The shooter then follows through, keeping his head down, like a golfer is taught to do.

There may also be occasions for a shooter to push the puck toward the net backhanded or to even try to lob it high in the air over a defenseman so it will bounce toward the goaltender. These are things to practice as you get better and better. But work on the wrist shot first. That is the most accurate. The slap shot may look more spectacular, but it isn't always as effective.

THE POSITIONS

One of the main differences in ice and roller hockey is the number of forwards in the game. Ice hockey has three; roller-hockey two. It is the forwards who will do the most hard skating during a game, often sprinting almost the full length of the rink, looking for breakaways and getting back quickly on defense. To be a forward you have to be in great shape and some kind of aerobic training is an absolute must.

The forwards must also be able to pass, receive passes, stickhandle and get that wrist shot off quickly. They must also be adept at handling face-offs. A face-off is how play begins and it is identical to that in ice hockey. The referee will drop the puck between two opposing players standing opposite each other. They will then try to control it and get the puck to one of their teammates.

There are almost always two sets of forwards on a roller-hockey team. No one player could skate an entire period without getting winded. Like ice hockey, the forward lines change on the fly, as the game continues, with two coming off and two more coming on.

Defensemen in roller hockey don't have to be quite as rugged as they do in ice hockey. That's because there is no checking or body contact allowed. Therefore, defensemen have to rely more on finesse and skating ability. They must be able to keep up with fast forwards and be adept at riding a player off the puck or having a quick enough stick to steal it.

Since defensemen often find themselves skating backward, they must try to get the puck or break up the play before the forwards really get rolling. No matter how good a skater, he cannot be going backwards and hope to keep up with an opponent who is skating forward. So be aggressive in pursuing the puck. A good defenseman cannot allow the forward to control him. He's got to either go after the puck or force a quick pass. If he allows too much stickhandling, he may find himself in trouble.

However, with just four skaters in the game at one time, defensemen must also develop offensive skills. They have to be ready to move the puck up the rink with all the skills of a forward. And they must practice their shooting, as well. Since defensemen often shoot from much further out than the forwards, they are more likely to use a slap shot to either score or cause a rebound that a forward might be able to put in the net.

There is one pitfall that defensemen can easily fall into. They

**24. (PHOTOS 24–26)
GOALIE IN THREE STOP
POSITIONS**

24.

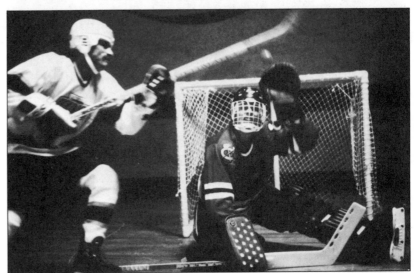

25.

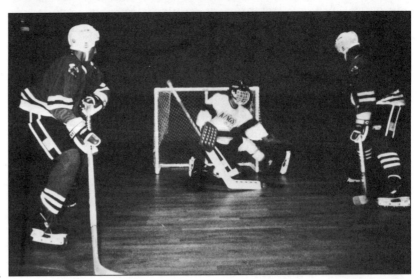

26.

cannot afford to forget about defense. Even if they are setting up the forwards or maneuvering for their own shot, they must remain aware of their opponents. With no offsides in rollerhockey, a forward can sneak down into his offensive zone long before the puck follows him. And if one of the defenseman doesn't get back, a rink length pass could leave the goaltender literally defenseless.

Like in ice hockey, rollerhockey goaltenders must have lightning quick reflexes and must be ready to use any means at their disposal to keep the puck out of the next. That may mean stopping it with their stick, grabbing it in their gloves hand, or stopping it by throwing their body in front of it and catching it on their skate or leg pads.

Rollerhockey goaltenders normally do not dive and sprawl as much as their ice hockey counterparts. The rollerhockey puck is made from weighted plastic and will glide smoothly on all types of surfaces. But it is lighter than an ice hockey puck, will curve, drop and rise more quickly, and will also rebound faster and more actively than an ice hockey puck. So rollerhockey goalies are instructed to only go to their knees or sprawl out when it is absolutely necessary to make a save. Otherwise, they should try to stay on their skates.

Goalies must be adept at moving back and forth on their skates in front of the net. They must follow the puck and give a shooter the smallest possible amount of open goal for which to shoot. This is called cutting down the angle. A goaltender should also not venture too far from his goal. If he skates out too far to recover a loose puck or to bring the puck up the rink, he may find it hard to get back if the other team suddenly steals the puck or intercepts a pass. And there is no greater embarrassment for a goalie than to be caught out of position so that his opponents get an easy, open-net goal.

STRATEGY

Strategy in rollerhockey differs somewhat from that of ice hockey, most of it dictated by the fact that there is one less player in the game. Many teams like to form either a box or a diamond when moving the puck up the rink. With the box, the forwards are up front and on the wings close to the sides of the rink. Both defensemen are further back and toward the middle. They try to move up the rink together, passing the puck and looking for a chance to break away.

It isn't until they get the puck deep in the defensive zone that they begin cutting and breaking toward the net, looking for a pass or a rebound from a long shot.

In the diamond formation, there are two players on the wings, one up front and another back deep. Some teams like to start with the box, then rotate into the diamond to confuse the defense. Both these formations usually require long accurate passes while bringing the puck up rink. It isn't until the attacking team is deep in the attacking zone that the passes shorten and the real cutting begins. It is down there that a player might use a quick backhand pass or drop pass.

However, teams do not automatically go into the box or the diamond. Many teams always look for the equivalent of the fast break in basketball. In rollerhockey, it's called breaking out. Once the defenseman has the puck behind his own net, his three teammates start up rink, the two forwards ahead, the other defenseman hanging back.

The player with the puck will look for a long pass, hoping one of the forwards has broken ahead of the opposing team's defense. He can also throw the puck into the attacking zone hoping a teammate will reach it before the defense or the opposing goaltender. Sometimes a defenseman will see the middle of the floor open and rush the puck up himself.

This is a more wide open game. It can result in a quick goal, but can also backfire if several offensive players get caught up ice. That's why teams don't use it all the time. Sometimes they will use the breakout to get into the attacking zone, then revert to the box or diamond, and begin the standard cutting toward the net.

Game plans usually don't vary too much. The best teams are those whose players have highly-developed individual skills and can put them together into a cohesive, smooth-working unit. But then again, this is the secret to almost every success-ful team in every sport.

The excitement of rollerhockey is building all over, just as the excitement of in-line skating continues to grow. If all the youngsters coming into this sport stay with it, continue to play rollerhockey and to race, there is a chance that these aspects of the sport could be open for professionals some day.

At the same time, the kids will always be out on the streets, as Bruce Jackson says, "ripping it up." They'll be doing more stunts, riding hills, doing half-pipes, jumping and making in-line skating the sport of the nineties.

ABOUT THE AUTHOR

BILL GUTMAN has been a freelance writer since 1972. In that time, he has written more than 100 books, many of them in the sports field. His work includes profiles and biographies of many sports stars, including recent works on Bo Jackson, Michael Jordan, David Robinson and Magic Johnson. In addition, Mr. Gutman has written biographies of such non-sports personalities as former president Andrew Jackson and jazz immortal Duke Ellington.

He has also written seven novels for youngsters—many of which have sports themes—as well as specialized high interest low vocabulary books. His adult books include the Magic Johnson biography, *Magic, More Than a Legend*; an autobiography with former New York Giants baseball star Bobby Thomson and recreation of the 1951 Giants-Dodgers pennant race called *The Giants Win the Pennant! The Giants Win the Pennant!*; a collection of profiles of former major league baseball stars called *When the Cheering Stops*, as well as several basketball and baseball histories.

Prior to *Blazing Bladers*, Mr. Gutman has written instructional "how-to" books on 12 different sports in a series entitled *Go For It!* He currently lives in Poughquag, N.Y., with his wife, Cathy, two stepchildren and a variety of pets.